THE
CROSSWOOD

THE
CROSSWOOD

GABRIELLE PRENDERGAST

orca currents

ORCA BOOK PUBLISHERS

Published in Canada and the United States in 2021 by Orca Book Publishers.
orcabook.com

Library and Archives Canada Cataloguing in Publication
Title: The crosswood / Gabrielle Prendergast.
Names: Prendergast, Gabrielle, author.
Series: Orca currents.
Description: Series statement: Orca Currents
Identifiers: Canadiana (print) 20200270370 | Canadiana (ebook) 20200270397 |
ISBN 9781459826625 (softcover) | ISBN 9781459826632 (PDF) |
ISBN 9781459826649 (EPUB)
Classification: LCC PS8631.R448 .C76 2021 | DDC jc813/.6—dc23

Library of Congress Control Number: 2020939209

Summary: In this high-interest accessible novel for middle-grade readers,
14-year-old Blue Jasper must enter the enchanted Crosswood when his
twin siblings are kidnapped by a Faerie king.

Orca Book Publishers is committed to reducing the consumption of
nonrenewable resources in the making of our books. We make
every effort to use materials that support a sustainable future.

Orca Book Publishers gratefully acknowledges the support for its publishing
programs provided by the following agencies: the Government of Canada,
the Canada Council for the Arts and the Province of British Columbia
through the BC Arts Council and the Book Publishing Tax Credit.

Edited by Tanya Trafford
Design by Ella Collier
Cover photograph by Getty Images/Donald Iain Smith
Author photo by Erika Forest

Printed and bound in Canada.

24 23 22 21 • 1 2 3 4

For Dylan and Ethan

Chapter One

It's quite comfortable here in the woodshed. With the door open it's not dark. And I found a nice log to sit on. I lean back on the dusty wall and look at the ceiling. Okay, there are a couple of spiders up there. That's not great. Outside, back at the house, I hear the screen door slam open.

"Blue! Blue? Where are you? I need help with the twins!"

The twins. My brother and sister. They are nearly ten. Their names are Indigo (a boy) and Violet (a girl). And they are, in my mother's words, "holy terrors." I don't see how that's my problem.

It is nearly dinnertime. I've spent most of the day chasing after the twins in the yard. I am over it. Over them and their antics. Indigo filled his pockets with beetles. I think he might have eaten one. Violet got sap in her hair and a pine needle in her eye. They both lost their socks. How do you lose socks in your own yard? I'll tell you. Somehow you throw them up into the tallest tree. If I lean out the woodshed door, I can still see them up there. Indigo's mismatched blue and white socks. Violet's red socks, one with a hole in the toe. I have no idea how they got them up there. Neither does Mom, even though she watched us all day from where she was building a chair on the porch.

"Blue, get back here! Indigo is in the rafters again!"

Mom never lets the twins out of her sight. She even homeschools them! I take the bus to the school in town. But the twins get to stay here in our cabin at the edge of the woods. I'm pretty sure they just run around all day. I don't think they learn much. But they don't need to. They're both weirdly smart. Unlike me. I'm weirdly average.

The twins are weirdly *weird*, actually. I know it's normal for little kids to have active imaginations but...wow. Indigo and Violet take it to new levels. They claim they're royalty. They tell me their real last name is Nash Panash Buckthorn Briar. It's not. It's Jasper, same as mine. They talk to fireflies. Only not in English. Not in any language I recognize. They speak it to each other too. Mom says that's normal for twins. But nothing is normal about Indigo and Violet. They drive me crazy.

"BLUE! Get in here NOW!"

I'm fourteen. I'm starting high school at the end of this summer. Ninth grade. I'm going to have enough stress. I'll have to take a new bus to a different town. I'll have to get up earlier. I'll probably have a ton more homework. I'm not going to have as much time to help with the twins. Mom is going to have to get used to that. I've tried to convince her to let Indigo and Violet go to school. But she won't listen. If they went to school, at least she'd have some time to herself. As it is, the only time she gets is after the twins go to sleep. And they only do that after being read about a hundred fairy tales.

I help out around the house. I sweep every day and wash the dishes. I even chop wood for our woodstove. Yep, we have a woodstove. Our little cabin is like something from another time. Sure, we have a proper toilet and electric lights, but that's about it. The woodstove is for cooking and heating. Our fridge runs off a solar battery. For entertainment we have books. No TV, no internet. To make a phone call Mom sends me up to the highway, where I can get a weak signal on her cell phone. A ten-minute walk. Five minutes if I run.

"Off-grid," Mom calls it. *Off-planet* is more like it.

It's just the four of us. Mom, the twins and me. No dad. My dad left when I was a baby. And the twins' dad…well, I don't even remember Mom being pregnant, so that shows how much I know.

I look up at the spiders again. They seem to judge me.

"I'm tired," I tell them. "I just needed a break."

The spiders are unimpressed. But so what? Spiders have hundreds of kids, and they usually get eaten by them. So they're not really a model of childcare I want to be aiming for.

Suddenly Mom screeches from the house. "No! Violet! Get down. Stop!" There's a huge crash. And another yell. Before I even think, I'm on my feet, out of the woodshed and running for the house.

Violet jumps when I burst through the back door. I mean, she really jumps. Somehow she ends up on top of the bookshelf. Indigo is above her, perched in the rafters like an owl. The dinner table is completely overturned. The dinner is on the floor. Dishes and mashed potatoes and lentil curry are everywhere. And in the middle of it sits Mom, clutching her ankle. Her face is twisted with pain.

"Mom! What happened?" I ask.

"Where were you? I told you I needed help with the twins!"

"Did they do this?" I'm suddenly so angry I want to break something. But it looks like there's nothing left to break. I turn toward the rafters and shout, "Indigo! Did you do this?"

"Violet was trying to catch me," he says quietly. He's not crying or anything, but I can tell he's upset. As bratty as they are, the twins love Mom.

I turn to Violet.

"Mom was trying to catch *me*," she says.

"Neither of you should have needed to be caught!" I yell. "Why can't you just settle down?"

"It's all right, Blue," Mom says.

"It's not all right!" I shout. "They're not chimps! They need to start acting like human beings!"

"But we're not human beings," Violet says sweetly.

"Enough!" I bellow, making her twitch. The bookshelf wobbles under her. "Enough of your fantasies! Look what you've done!"

I'm furious now. I know it's partly because I'm worried about Mom. But I'm also really mad at the twins for always being so…wild. For taking up all of Mom's time. All of her attention. For the first four years of my life, it was just me and her. We were doing great. I had started preschool. Mom was studying. She was going to go back to work. Then these two lunatics came along and ruined everything. Including tonight's dinner.

Indigo swings under the rafters and seems to float down to the floor. Violet jumps from the bookshelf and lands as softly as a cat. They stand in front of me, holding hands.

"We're sorry, Blue," they say together.

I want to rant at them some more, but Mom whimpers as she tries to get up.

"Can you stand?" I ask.

"I don't think so," she says, holding her ankle again. "I think it's just sprained though. Take the phone up to the road. Call Mrs. Chen. She can drive us to the clinic. We'll get pizza in town."

The twins start to cheer but stop when I glare at them.

"You two," I say, grabbing Mom's phone. "If you don't clean up this mess by the time I'm back…"

They both open their eyes wide. But I can't think of any way to threaten them. And I don't really want to. They might be monsters, but they're annoyingly cute. And I can't help but love them.

"If you *do* clean this up by the time I come back," I say instead, "I'll read you the first chapter of *The Hobbit*."

Then the little brats *do* cheer.

Chapter Two

It turns out Mom's ankle is broken. It's just a hairline fracture. But it is enough to make Indigo and Violet calm down for a few days. I think they are actually ashamed. That's progress.

Truth is, I'm ashamed too. If I hadn't been hiding in the woodshed, the accident would never have happened. I'm paying for it too. Even though Mom got a walking cast, she has to take things slow. The twins don't really do slow. So it's me who has to run around chasing them. After a week of this, I'm exhausted. Finally Mom relents. She lets the twins listen to an audiobook on her old tape player.

I'd really like to take a nap. But the house is a mess. And Mom's ankle hurts. She sits with it propped up on a pillow. The twins lie on the floor at her feet, headphones on, kicking each other. At least they're quiet.

I grab a broom and sweep the kitchen. I quickly do the dishes. I gather some clothes and towels off the floor and drop them in the laundry basket. When that's done I sit with Mom for a few minutes. The twins are playing with a long piece of knitting yarn while they listen to the story. They tie and tangle it into impossibly intricate knots and webs. I watch for a while, trying to figure out what to say to Mom.

"Maybe the twins could go to a day camp," I try.

Mom just laughs.

"Seriously. There's a sports camp at the community center. They could run around all day."

"That would end in tears," Mom says. "And blood. And neither of them coming from the twins."

I look down at the twins on the floor. Violet has tied Indigo's wrist to the chair leg with the yarn. Her ankle is tied to his knee. One of his toes is tied to one of her braids. They don't seem worried about it, so I decide to leave them for now. At least they can't run around this way.

"What about school?" I ask. "Maybe they could start at school in September?"

"Blue," Mom says. "The twins are fine here with me. Regular school wouldn't work for them. They're too..."

"Smart?" I ask. "They have a gifted class at school." I always wanted to be in the gifted class. Unfortunately I wasn't smart enough.

"Special," Mom says. "The twins are too special."

She doesn't mean special as in disabled. The twins aren't disabled. If anything, they have *more* abilities than most kids. She means special as in weird. It seems unfair to me that weird kids can't go to school. Actually, I think weird kids *should* go to school. If there had been a few more weird kids at my school, I might have had a better time.

I *was* the weird kid at my school. I only hope high school will be different.

Suddenly I don't want to talk about the twins anymore. I'd love to talk about my own problems. My worries about going to high school. The fact that I have hardly any friends. That I need new clothes. That I'm starting to grow a mustache and I don't know how to shave.

Mom never has time to listen to my problems. Whenever I try to tell her something, one of the twins interrupts. By the time she gets them into bed at night, she's too tired. Sometimes I wish the twins would just disappear. Not forever or anything. Just for a day or two.

I turn back to Mom. She's busy stopping Indigo from winding the yarn around his own neck. She doesn't even notice me.

The audiobook only works for an hour. Before long the twins are jumping from the back porch down onto the lawn. Mom watches them uneasily, her fingers gripping the railing.

"I don't want another broken bone in this house."

I think that's unlikely. Neither of the twins has ever broken anything. They've jumped out of trees, out of windows and once out of the back of a moving truck. It was moving slowly, but still. They never even get sick. I was sick all the time when I was little. I was so sick I had to be in the hospital for a month around the time the twins were born. Maybe that's why I don't remember Mom being pregnant.

"Why don't I take them for a walk?" I suggest. Walking is safer than jumping off things, at least.

"I'm not really up for a walk n—" Mom starts. But Violet interrupts her.

"Yes! Let's go into the woods!"

"Yes!" Indigo agrees. "I want to look for slugs!"

I hesitate to ask what plans he has for the slugs.

"I'll take them, Mom. You can stay here."

"No!" she says a little sharply. "I'll come. We just have to go a bit slow."

Like I said, the twins don't really do slow.

They run through the yard to the path leading into the woods behind our house. I chase after them, with Mom limping behind me.

"Wait!" I yell. "Slow down!"

By the time I catch up to the twins, Mom is far behind us. I manage to get them to walk slowly so she can catch up. The forest is quiet and smells like earth and leaves. The path is one we've walked many times. But it seems especially beautiful today. Maybe it's just seeing the twins bouncing along in their bright clothes. They seem so at home here. Like they belong.

I turn to see how Mom is doing behind us. When I turn back, the twins bounce off the path and into the trees.

"Hey! Wait!"

I chase after them, barely aware of Mom's frantic cries behind me.

There's a rough path where they turned. I've never noticed it before. It winds through tall, twisted trees. I catch a glimpse of Violet's golden braids just disappearing into the dense green branches.

"Catch them, Blue!" Mom yells. I don't look back. I can hear the fear in her voice. I don't really understand why she's so scared. This forest isn't dangerous. Is it? Surely the twins will stop or come back eventually. Won't they? Something fills me with fear too.

I push through the trees, sharp branches scratching at me. I can't even see the twins anymore. Not their colorful clothes. Not their bright blond hair. Nothing.

"Indigo! Violet! Come back!" I yell. The thick blanket of leaves above me absorbs my voice. "COME BACK!"

Suddenly the forest starts to spin. It's as though the ground is moving under my feet. The air gets thick, and everything seems to slow down. And a weird smell drifts around me. A sweet smell. I can hear Mom's voice, now faint and far away. Over her voice I can just hear the twins laughing happily. But then it stops. It's as though a recording has been turned off with a switch.

The twins were here only a second ago. Now they're gone.

Chapter Three

I can hear Mom yelling through the blood pounding in my ears. The forest has stopped spinning. Now, apart from Mom's voice, it is deathly quiet. Desperate, I tear at the undergrowth. I search under shrubs and bushes and rotting logs. There are half a dozen places for two small kids to hide. But I don't find them.

"INDIGO! VIOLET!" I yell. But there's nothing except my voice bouncing off the trees.

I spin when I hear a crunch behind me. It's only Mom.

"They were right here!" I wail before she even says anything. "They were only ten feet away."

"What happened?" she asks. Her face is set and hard. Like stone.

"They just vanished," I say helplessly. "I could hear them and then…"

"What? What?" Mom prods.

"It was weird," I say, feeling tears prickling the back of my eyes. "It was like I *felt* them disappear."

I expect Mom to start yelling at me or telling me I'm crazy, but she just frowns.

"How did it feel?" she asks. "You said you felt something? What was it?"

I close my eyes for a second and try to think back. It feels like trying to remember something that happened a long time ago. But it was only a few seconds ago. I think something is wrong with my brain.

"It was like the air pressure changed," I say. "My ears popped or something. Like when we drive up the mountain."

Mom nods. "Did you see anything?"

I open my eyes and look at the place where I last caught sight of Violet. "I saw both of the twins turn onto this path. Indigo was in front of Violet. I saw them run down the path, past this tree." I point to a particularly spiky, twisted tree.

Mom limps in a circle around the tree, examining it. I check it out too. It seems out of place somehow. Like it's too old for this forest. Or the wrong kind of tree. The color of its leaves is slightly off. Instead of the fresh yellowy green of the other trees, it's dark green. Like emeralds. And the bark is nearly black. Worst of all, the branches are covered with thorns.

"What kind of tree is this?" I ask.

Mom doesn't answer. She looks back at the little path the twins took. It seems to end right here where we're standing.

"Did you see anything else?" Mom asks. "Anything out of the ordinary?"

I feel strange telling her. I don't want her to think I've gone crazy. "The forest was spinning," I say finally.

"Spinning? Did you smell anything?" Mom asks.

It's a strange question. But I do remember smelling something. Something thick and...

"Sweet," I say. "It was like..."

"Strawberry jam?" Mom asks.

"Yes! Did you smell it too?"

"No," she says. She doesn't explain further. Because suddenly the air fills with that smell again. Like strawberry jam, only different. Almost like strawberry perfume, if there is such a thing. It's so strong that my eyes start to water.

The forest doesn't spin as much this time. Or maybe it's me who doesn't spin because I have the sense to hold on to the tree. But my ears pop again, and my vision goes really blurry. When I blink and get back to normal, I'm grateful to see that Mom is still here. She's staring over my right shoulder. Her eyes and mouth are open in shock.

I turn around slowly, afraid of what I'm going to see.

Standing behind me, as though she appeared out of nowhere, is a woman I can only describe as a queen.

She is wearing a crown. That's the first clue. And it's not a little sparkly tiara thing like brides sometimes wear with their veils. It's a massive golden crown. It's covered in gemstones of every color. It looks like it is made of twigs wound together and then dipped in gold. The woman's hair underneath the crown is golden too. It tumbles down in curls and waves to her waist. She looks about Mom's age.

Her clothes are amazing. She's wearing a red dress that drapes down to her feet. It's decorated with sparkling jewels and embroidery. Over the dress she wears a purple cloak. It's lined with white fur and trimmed with more jewels. She has a bunch of diamond necklaces strung around her neck and rings on every finger.

Her face might be beautiful, but she's so angry it's hard to tell.

Just as my eyes adjust to all the color and sparkle, two men step out from the trees behind her. Both are wearing some kind of armor, like knights. And they have swords slung from their waists.

I take a step back, pulling Mom with me.

"Juliette Jasper!" the strange woman says. Her voice makes the leaves around us vibrate. I have to remind myself that Juliette Jasper is my mother. Everyone calls her Jules.

"Juliette Jasper!" the queen repeats. "You have broken our pact!"

"They just vanished," Mom says. "Can you find them? Can you help us search?"

"There is no need to search," the woman says. "I know where they are."

"Where are they?" Mom asks.

"That is no longer your concern," the woman says. "Your concern now is our pact and the price you must pay for breaking it."

I can't just stand here in silence anymore. "What is going on?" I ask. "Who are you?"

The woman looks at me like I'm a bug she's about to squash.

"Who are you?" she asks, narrowing her eyes.

"I'm Blue Jasper. Indigo and Violet's brother."

The woman sniffs. "I am Olea of Nearwood. Indigo and Violet's mother."

I look at Mom. Her hand is over her mouth.

"Uh, I'm pretty sure *this* is their mom," I say. "*My* mom. The twins' mom. I'm their brother."

Olea stares at me again. There's so much anger in her face that I pull Mom behind me.

"You are not important," Olea says.

"Now just a minute—" Mom starts, but Olea interrupts her.

"SILENCE!" she shouts. The guys with swords move toward us.

I'm starting to think that maybe I fell and hit my head. Can this be real? It feels like a dream. Or a nightmare.

Olea steps forward. "I am Olea, queen of the Faerie kingdom of Nearwood, and the twins, the ones your mother calls 'Indigo' and 'Violet', are my children."

"What's Nearwood?" I ask stupidly.

Olea glares at Mom. "You haven't told this human boy? You haven't told him who the twins really are?"

Mom sighs. "No," she says. "I haven't told him anything."

I turn around to look at her. "Mom?" I say, feeling goose bumps rising on my skin. "Is this real?"

"I'm sorry, Blue," she says. "Yes, it's real. It's all real."

Chapter Four

This time my head spins, because I think I'm about to faint. Mom puts her arm around me, pulling me close.

"It's going to be okay," she says.

I pull away from her. "No it's not!" I say. "Where are Indigo and Violet? What is this pact?"

Mom is strangely calm. She turns to Olea, speaking slowly.

"Will you let me explain this to my son?"

Olea narrows her eyes.

"Address me properly," she says through her teeth.

Mom actually goes down on one knee. She bows her head. "Forgive me, Your Majesty. Will you permit me time to explain everything to my son?"

Olea flicks her eyes to me. I feel an irresistible tug and find myself falling to my knees too. The damp forest floor soaks my jeans. I lower my eyes, which means I don't exactly see what happens next. But when I glance up, Olea is sitting on an ornate throne. In addition to the two armed guards, there are two young women with Olea now. One of them feeds her brightly colored fruit. The other one fans her with a feathered fan. They are both dressed in long yellow gowns.

"You may begin," Olea says.

Mom takes a deep breath. I think I've forgotten how to breathe.

"Remember when you were sick?" Mom asks. "Around the time the twins were born?"

"I remember the hospital," I say. "I also remember some weird things. But you always said that was the fever."

"Some of it probably was the fever," Mom says. "But some of it might not have been."

"This is boring," Olea says. "Get to the good part."

Mom closes her eyes for a second. "The truth is… you were so sick I thought you might die. I was driving you to the hospital in the rain. I was driving too fast. The car slid off the road. We got stuck in the mud."

"It *was* raining quite hard, wasn't it?" Olea says lightly. "I do like rain."

I guess my brush with death doesn't mean that much to her.

"It was late," Mom says. "It was the middle of the night. There was no one on the road."

"It was *deliciously* dark," Olea says.

Mom ignores her. "I had to carry you," she says. "You were so small. It wasn't hard. But taking the road was the long way. It was still a mile to the bridge.

I knew I could walk through the woods to the river. There was a footbridge right up to the highway. I could flag someone down there."

"I don't remember any of this," I say.

"Oh, Blue," Mom says. "You were so sick. I'm not surprised."

"Boring. Boring," Olea says, waving her hand. "Human sickness is so dull. Tell him about the forest."

Mom frowns, but she goes on. "Right," she says. "The forest. It was much darker than I realized. I wasn't thinking straight, of course. I was so worried about you. And it was wet and slippery. I slipped down a bank. I got scratched by thorns. Then I must have made a wrong turn. I was lost. I never found the footbridge. I never found the river."

Mom falls silent and stares at the ground. The look on her face tells me she's remembering. Remembering getting lost in the rain at night. Remembering me being so sick she thought I would die. I reach over and take her hand.

"What *did* you find?" I ask.

Olea chuckles, a low and creepy laugh. "She found me, Blue Jasper," she says.

→ ★ ←

Mom squeezes my hand, ducking her head again.

"If it pleases Your Majesty," she says, "you could tell the rest of the story."

Olea leans back in her throne. She rolls her eyes.

"I suppose," she says. "That would certainly be more interesting."

Then we all wait while she eats several pieces of fruit. Her servant fans her. I think if Olea would only take off her fur cloak, she wouldn't need fanning. I'm starting to feel impatient by the time she speaks again.

"My twins had just been born," Olea says. "And I had spirited them through the Crosswood into the human world."

"What's the Crosswood?" I ask.

Olea wrinkles her nose as though she smells something bad. "The Crosswood is a wood, like this one." She waves her hand at the twisted trees. They seem more magical and less ordinary the longer we stay here. "In every wood there are places like this. Here the magic that upholds the border between human and Faerie realms is thin. There is a kind of..." Her voice trails off as she searches for the word. "A kind of mirror," she finishes. "There is a mirror version of this place in the Faerie realm. That is the Crosswood."

"So a Crosswood has two sides?" I ask. "A human side and a Faerie side?"

Olea frowns at me. Even though I suspect I've got it right, she looks disappointed.

"You are clever for a human," she says. "Are you sure you don't have Faerie blood?"

"He doesn't," Mom says.

Olea stares at me for a few seconds. It's like she's trying to analyze my blood herself. She shrugs.

"As I was saying," she continues, "I had spirited my twins into the human world. I needed somewhere to hide them."

"Why?" I ask.

"They were not safe in the Faerie realm," she says.

"Why not?"

"You're so smart, human," she snaps. "Why don't you tell me?"

"Someone was after them?" I try.

Olea's eyes widen for a second. Then she crosses her arms and looks away, making a *humph* noise.

"Well. That's correct," she says with a sneer. "Oren, the King of Farwood, was after them. He has always hated Nearwood and hated me. But a treaty between the Woods means that by Faerie law he cannot enter my kingdom to harm me."

"The twins aren't covered by that law?" I ask.

"No," Olea says. "Faerie children are very rare. We didn't think to put that in the treaty."

I look over at Mom. She's wiping a tear from her cheek.

"So...the king of Farwood has the twins now?" I ask.

Mom nods. "I tried to—" she starts, but Olea interrupts her.

"You have failed in your task," she says angrily. "You have broken our pact. Payment must be made in blood!"

My heart drops. "Wait, what?" I yell. "What kind of pact was this? What do you mean *payment in blood?*"

Mom lets go of my hand and sits back on her heels. She looks tired.

"I was desperate, Blue," she says. "You were barely breathing. And I...I made the terrible mistake of asking her for help."

"Which I provided, of course," Olea says. "For I am a good queen. I flew you, Blue Jasper, and your mother to the—" She turns to one of her servants. "What is the word?"

"Hospital," the servant whispers.

Olea looks very impressed with herself. "I flew you to the *hotpizal*. The human healers did their sad little magic tricks on you. Then you got better." She shrugs. The woods fall silent for a moment.

"We *flew*?" I ask as that detail sinks in.

"Indeed," Olea says. She raises her eyebrows at me. For an instant, behind her back, I catch a glimpse of a huge set of green, bat-like wings. But in an eye blink they are gone.

"W-where does this pact come in?" I ask, gathering myself.

Olea laughs. "Your mother was so grateful," she says. "What did you say, Juliette Jasper?"

Mom hangs her head. "I don't remember," she says.

Olea laughs even harder. "Ah, it's so delightful the way you humans can lie. So amusing." Her laughing stops abruptly, and her mood darkens. "I remember exactly what you said, Juliette Jasper."

Mom cringes. I put my arm around her.

When Olea speaks, her voice sounds just like Mom's. It's like a recording.

" 'Thank you! My son owes you his life. How can I ever repay you?' " Olea says.

Her servants giggle. Even the grim-faced guards smirk.

Olea's voice returns to normal. "Then I said, 'You can keep my twins safe.' And your mother said, 'Ummm, for how long?' and I said, 'For as long as you want your son to live,' and then—"

"Wait! What?" I yell.

"I'm sorry, Blue," Mom says. "That's what I agreed."

Olea seems pretty pleased for someone whose kids have been kidnapped. "Faerie law is magically enforced," she explains calmly. "You have twenty-four hours. Then I'm afraid the terms of the pact will apply."

"What does that mean?" I ask. I can't believe this is happening.

"It means, Blue Jasper," Olea says, "that if the twins aren't safe by sunset tomorrow, you die."

Chapter Five

"Take me instead!" Mom says immediately.

"If you wish," Olea says lightly.

"Wait, no!" I yell. But the trees tremble. The air around us ripples. I get the feeling that some sort of spell has just been invoked. Or changed. "You can't just trade Mom's life for mine."

Olea looks at me, perplexed. "I'm not a monster, Blue Jasper," she says. "I don't want to see a child die.

Your mother's life was a fair trade. I accepted it. The Woods accepted it."

"But can't you just cancel the pact altogether?"

For the first time, Olea shows some regret. It makes her face look almost human for a second. But it passes quickly.

"Faerie magic doesn't work like that, I'm afraid," she says. "It would pain me to see you lose your mother. But a pact is a pact. Lives can be traded—it's true. But the price of a broken Faerie pact must be paid. The magic of the Faerie Woods will uphold that law whether I like it or not."

"There must be something we can do!" I yell. My ears are ringing. I feel like I'm going to faint again.

"You can get the twins back," Olea says.

Right now nothing would make me happier than to have the twins back. I feel terrible for having wished they would disappear for a few days. And not just because of Mom. I'm worried about them too. What is this King Oren planning to do with them?

They could be hurt. They're probably scared. I need to save them.

"Can you tell me exactly how the pact was supposed to work?" I ask. I feel like one of those lawyers in a suspense novel. I'm trying to find a loophole. Some way of getting us out of this. "How was my mom, a human, supposed to protect the twins from a magical Faerie king?"

Olea sighs. "It's quite simple. You humans have no magic of your own, of course," she says. "But Faerie magic can be put on you. Even in ways that might not work with Faeries. So I put a protective spell on your mother. If the twins were within range of her hearing, nothing from the Faerie realm could touch them. As long as the twins were safe, the pact was upheld."

I turn and stare at Mom. So this was why she'd rarely let the twins out of her sight. Why she wouldn't leave the house even if the twins were fast asleep in bed. Why she'd never sent them to school.

She'd done it for me. To protect *me*. And I'd messed that up. I'd let the twins run off. And now I'd let Mom exchange her life for mine. Suddenly my mother seems small and fragile. Like she's the child and I'm the grown-up.

I look back at Olea.

"Can't you go and rescue the twins?" I ask. "You're a Faerie. You're magical."

Olea seems suddenly to tire of being fanned. She shoves her servant away.

"I would if I could," she says impatiently. "The treaty means that no Nearwood Faerie can enter Farwood without being invited. It goes the other way too, obviously. And neither of us is inclined to issue invitations."

"But if the Faeries can't enter each other's kingdoms, why didn't you keep the twins with you in Nearwood?" I ask. "They would have been safe there."

Olea pinches her lips. "There are creatures other than Faeries in the Woods," she says. "Oren could have paid any of them to harm the twins. And protective spells like the one I used on your mother don't work on Faeries or in the Faerie Woods at all. I needed a human. I needed to leave the twins in the human world."

I put the idea of "creatures other than Faeries" out of my head for the moment. I could worry about that later.

"Okay, so no Nearwood Faerie can enter Farwood," I repeat. "What about a human? Can a human enter Farwood without an invitation?"

"Blue, no," Mom says.

But Olea raises her eyebrows at me. "Humans who stumble into the Faerie Woods rarely stumble out," she says.

"If I save the twins, Mom won't die, right?"

She nods. "If Indigo and Violet are safe, the pact is upheld. Your mother's life will be hers again."

"You promise?"

"I have no need to promise. The Faerie Woods will uphold the law. But for my part, yes, I promise. All I care about is…" She pauses, seeming to struggle. "The twins being back with your family."

I turn to Mom. "I have to try," I say. "I'll find them and bring them back somehow."

"I'll come with you," Mom says.

"No," I say. "You'll just slow me down. You can barely walk."

"But—"

"No!" I say firmly. "It's my fault they ran off. It's my responsibility to get them back."

When I look again at Olea, she's smiling at me. Not a friendly smile. A sneaky smile. Like she knows something. I don't trust her. But I shake that feeling off, because I'm going to need her help.

"Can you take me into the Faerie Woods? Get me close to Farwood?"

"I can," Olea says, admiring her colorful fingernails.

After a moment she continues. "What will you give me?"

"Oh no you don't!" Mom says, suddenly bold. "We've had enough of your deals, Olea of Nearwood."

Olea pouts a bit, but she shrugs. "Fine. I'll take you into the Crosswood. You'll have to find your way from there. Say goodbye to your mother."

Mom stands, and we hug. I realize I'm nearly as tall as her. When did that happen?

"Be careful, Blue," she says, holding me by the shoulders. "Don't eat or drink anything Faeries give you. Um...don't dance to their music. And don't make any deals. Remember that above all. Deals made with Faeries rarely turn out well."

"Got it," I say.

Mom slips off her hoodie and gives it to me. I put it on, even though it's purple and flowery. It fits me quite well. I guess we *are* nearly the same size.

"There are two granola bars in the pocket," she says. "And a juice box."

Mom always carries snacks on her for the twins. I'm grateful for that right now.

"Be careful," she says, kissing my cheek.

"I will," I say.

"This is tedious," Olea says. "Follow me."

I step away from Mom. Olea is already walking with her servants into the twisted trees. The throne has disappeared. I turn back for a last look at Mom as I reach the trees. She's standing there, watching us. Crying. I have to bite my lip not to cry too.

Then the forest spins again. The trees seem to reach down and encircle me with their branches. They push me down onto the ground. The roots of the trees twist around me, pulling me into the earth. I taste dirt in my mouth. For a second I can't breathe or move. It's like I've been buried alive. I try to struggle against it, but I'm being crushed.

Then I feel someone tugging down on my ankle. I stop struggling. I sink and sink until finally I pop out of the earth like a cork. Spitting dirt, I roll over and realize I'm upside down. Or the world is upside down. I seem to be on the underside of the forest. The moment I think that, my mind flips everything, and I'm right way up again. I'm lying on the ground in a clearing surrounded by twisted trees. It looks just like the clearing where I lost the twins. But I know it's not.

Olea is looking down at me, an amused expression on her face. "Welcome to the Crosswood, Blue Jasper," she says.

Chapter Six

I look around. The first thing I notice is the color. It's deeper. Every green leaf and brown branch and red berry looks like it's made from expensive silk. Even the dark turned-up earth I just crawled out of is like black velvet. Above me I can see the sky through the branches. It appears to be twilight. I don't know how I'm going to survive when darkness falls. I need to find Farwood. And fast.

"Which way is it?" I ask. "Farwood?"

Olea's servants chuckle. "There are many ways out of the Crosswood," Olea says. "The important thing is to find the right one. It would be a shame if you accidentally fell through the wrong one."

Now her servants laugh, holding their sides.

"What does that mean?" I ask.

Olea glares at her servants, and they fall silent.

"The Crosswood allows you to return to the human realm. But not all exits return you to the same place. You might end up in—where is that cold place?"

"Siberia?" one of her servants offers.

"Yes, Siberia," Olea says. "Or Toronto."

"So how do I find the right one?"

Olea's servants drift away. I watch, astonished, as each of them flickers and slips into the ground. They disappear like snakes into holes.

"There are Faeries in the Crosswood who don't belong to my court or the court of King Oren," Olea says. "One of them can help you." She turns and takes a step. Her body shimmers.

"Wait!" I say. "How can I find them?"

But there's a flash and a strong smell of strawberries, and then she's gone.

I stand there for a few seconds, breathing hard. Olea's mention of "creatures other than Faeries" comes back to me now. That could mean anything! I have no weapons. I have no idea which way to go. All I have are two granola bars and a juice box.

My only hope is to find another Faerie before darkness falls. I peer through the trees. There's nothing but forest in every direction. Just as I'm about to give up, I see something. A little flash of light in the distance. It moves.

A person? Someone with a lantern? I almost yell, but I hesitate. What if they're not friendly? I decide to sneak up on them instead.

I arm myself with a long, broken branch and tiptoe through the trees. At least if I get attacked I'll have some chance. It briefly occurs to me that I must look like a wizard with a staff.

When I get closer to the light, I realize that's all it is. A light just floating there.

It looks like a firefly bobbing in front of my face. Suddenly it whizzes off. I follow it for what feels like a long time. But I don't get anywhere. Finally the light stops by another twisted tree. It hovers there for a moment. Then it disappears into a crack in the trunk.

"Hey! Wait!" I say.

Suddenly something tackles me. I crash onto the forest floor. Without thinking, I roll over and swing my wizard staff. It makes a loud crack as it hits whatever tackled me.

"Ow!"

I barely dodge a webbed foot flying in my face.

A *webbed* foot? Am I fighting with a frog? I scramble away. Turning back, I raise my staff, ready to strike.

At first there doesn't seem to be anything there. But then part of the mossy undergrowth moves. It sits up.

"Lily pads, that hurt," the creature says, raising a webbed hand to rub the side of its head.

"What...?" I start. "Who are you?"

"I'm Salix," it says.

I raise my staff again as Salix stands. It's not a frog. Salix appears to be a boy about my age. A green boy. His hair is like grass growing from the top of his head. His face is a pale green, like the inside of a cucumber. And his clothes seem to be woven out of fern leaves.

"Put down your stick," he says, irritated. "I'm not going to hurt you."

"Why did you tackle me then?"

"Ugh," Salix says. "Humans. I tackled you because I was afraid you were going to follow that Will-o'-the-Wisp into the tree. That crossing comes out in a grizzly bear's den. That would not be good for you. What's your name?"

"Blue," I say. "Blue Jasper."

Salix widens his large yellow eyes. "You're Blue Jasper? The foster brother of the prince and princess of Nearwood?"

It feels weird to be called their foster brother, but I nod. I'm still getting over the grizzly-bear thing. "So you've heard of me?" I ask.

Salix reaches forward and pulls me upright. Then he shakes my hand so vigorously I nearly fall over.

"Of course I've heard of you. Everyone in the Crosswood has!"

I look down at our hands as he lets go of me.

"Are you a…Faerie?"

"Sort of," Salix says. "I'm a Nixie. Kind of like a water Faerie."

That explains the webbing.

"So if you know about Indigo and Violet, then you must know they've been kidnapped," I say.

"What?" Salix's large eyes get even larger. "When did that happen?"

"About an hour ago," I say. "King Oren of Farwood has them. I have to get them back or my mother's broken pact will mean she dies."

Salix cringes. "Oh no. A pact with Queen Olea?"

I nod. "I'm going to do everything I can to sneak into Farwood and get the twins back," I say. "But I need help."

"Flippers," Salix says, shaking his head. "Who in the Faerie Woods would be silly enough to help you do *that*?" His laugh stops abruptly when he notices me staring at him. "No," he says firmly.

"Please."

"King Oren hates me," Salix says. "I dripped pond water on his favorite rug, and mushrooms grew there."

"I'm sure he's forgotten about that," I try.

"It was last week."

"He's probably had the rug cleaned by now."

Salix rolls his eyes. "You really don't know how Faerie mushrooms work, do you?"

"No," I admit, and though I'm very curious to learn, I need to focus. I can learn all about this weird world later. I reach into my pocket. "Here." I hold out a granola bar. "If you help me, you can have this."

"Ew! No thank you." Salix wrinkles his nose.

I pull out the juice box. "How about this?"

He examines the juice and smiles. "Yes, all right then. I'll help you get to Farwood if you agree to give me something."

"Yes, okay, fine," I say. I try to hand him the juice.

"I don't want that," he says.

The trees around us shimmer as I realize what I've done. I've agreed to give him "something" if he helps me. Not a juice box. Just *something*. I'm an idiot.

I've just made a deal with a Faerie, and I don't even know what it's for.

Chapter Seven

"You tricked me!" I say.

"Can I still have the juice?" Salix asks as we start walking.

"No!" I say, popping the straw into the top of the juice box. I take an exaggerated sip.

Salix actually looks remorseful. "I'm sorry," he says. "It's the Faerie way. It's hard to resist."

"What is this 'something' going to be?"

"I don't know," Salix says. "But I promise it won't be bad."

I try to make the juice seem as tasty as possible while I ignore him.

This forest seems to go on forever. The sun has now gone down completely. Salix has a tiny lantern that is surprisingly bright. If not for it we'd be walking in the dark.

Salix sighs. "Well, if I'm going to help you properly, I suppose I could teach you some things about Faeries."

I tuck the empty juice box back into my pocket. "Like what?" I ask.

"Helpful things," Salix says. "Things to help keep you safe. Like...well, for example, you should know that Faeries can't lie."

"You can't?" I say. "So if I asked you to say, 'Salix is a bloated baboon,' you couldn't do it?"

"No," he says. "Could you say that?"

"Salix is a bloated baboon."

He frowns at me. "I deserved that," he says.

"What else can you tell me about Faeries?" I ask.

"Faeries have very long full names," Salix says.

"How is that helpful?"

"If you know a Faerie's full name, and you use it to command them, they have to give you three wishes. You can even make them do magic things. Or things that seem impossible."

"Wait," I say. "So if I had said to my brother, 'Indigo Nash Panash Buckthorn Briar, I command you to clean the bathroom,' he would have done it? That would be magic."

"Yes," Salix says. "But it only works three times. And only for humans."

"I'm going to remember that when I find him and Violet," I say. "That reminds me of something I've been curious about. Why do their names match mine?"

"What do you mean?" Salix asks.

"Like, my name is Blue, and they're Indigo and Violet. Our names go together. They're from the colors of the rainbow. Red, orange, yellow, green, Blue, Indigo and Violet. But if I'm not their real brother, why do we match?"

Salix grins. "I heard it was because Olea forgot to name them," he says. "She was in such a hurry to get them out of the Faerie Woods that she forgot to give them names. When your mother asked what their names were, Olea told her to pick something!"

I think about that for a while. It seems strange that Olea would have forgotten to name her own children, but she's a strange…woman. And it makes sense that Mom would have chosen matching names. Even though we don't match. I look nothing like Indigo and Violet. I have brown hair and dark eyes. They have blond hair and light blue eyes. Maybe Mom thought the names would make us seem more like real siblings.

I get sad thinking about it. I miss those rotten little monsters.

⇒ ★ ⇐

"How much farther is it?" I ask after another hour passes. We don't seem to have gotten anywhere.

Salix stops and stares into the distance ahead of us.

"About three or four days, I think," he says.

"Three or four *days*?! But I have to get the twins back by tomorrow at sunset."

"Flippers!" Salix says. "Why didn't you say so? We'll have to fly."

"Fly?" I ask. I've never flown before. Not that I remember anyway. Not even in a plane. "Can't you just…Olea and her servants just kind of disappeared."

"That's because they are Nearwood Faeries," Salix says. "Any Faerie can slip into their own wood with magic. But they can't slip into other woods. Not unless they're invited."

"And you can't slip into woods?"

"No," Salix says a little sadly. "I'm not part of any wood."

"Why not?"

He looks away for a second. I regret asking the question. It clearly upsets him.

"My wood disappeared," he says at last. "Or at least the way into it did. It's hard to explain." He looks a little irritated. "We don't have time."

"Sorry," I say. "Can you fly?"

"I can't, no. But I know someone who can."

He turns off the path, and we start to head downhill. After a few minutes we arrive at a pond. In the dark it's hard to see how large it is. Weeds and vines hang down around us. The whole thing is a little spooky. I can hear the water lapping a bit. But I can't see anything. What is in there? One of the "creatures other than Faeries" that live in the Crosswood?

Salix puts his fingers up to his teeth and whistles. "Finola!" he calls out. "Finola, are you here?"

I see something move in the distance, on the other side of the pond. Something white and ghostly glides toward us. I step back into the cover of trees and vines. But as the thing gets closer, I realize it's a swan. A *giant* swan. It swims right up to Salix and nibbles at his knee.

"Hello, Finola," he says. "Still stuck in swan form, I see."

The swan nods. She flicks her head at me as I emerge from the trees.

"That's Blue," Salix says. "He's human and the foster brother of Princess Violet and Prince Indigo. They've been kidnapped by King Oren of Farwood."

Finola opens her beak like she's shocked. I have to cough back a laugh.

"This is Finola MacLear," Salix says. "She was cursed by a bog witch a few months ago, and now she's stuck as a swan."

"That's…um…unfortunate," I say. I feel foolish talking to a swan, but I guess that's life in Faerie land. "It's nice to meet you."

Finola nods at me.

"Finola," Salix says. "We need a favor. Blue needs to get the prince and princess back before sundown tomorrow or his mother will die. Can you fly us to Farwood Castle? You're able to go over the mountains instead of around them."

Finola looks at each of us as if she's measuring us up. Then she nods.

We step back as she clambers out of the pond. She shakes herself, spraying water everywhere. She flicks her head toward her back. Salix climbs on first, straddling Finola's back like she's a horse. Actually, now that I'm near her, I can see she's nearly as big as a horse. I get up behind Salix.

"Hold on," he says.

I grab his shoulders. Finola spreads her wings. She turns back to the pond. My feet get soaked as she takes off. She half runs, half flies just above the water. At the very last second before I think we'll go crashing into the dark trees, she lifts off.

We're flying!

Chapter Eight

Finola starts to descend just as the sun peeks over the horizon. The flight wasn't too terrible. That is, I only barfed once. Not bad for my first time. Soon we're sailing just above the treetops. I can see the tall towers of a castle in the distance. I never thought I'd see a castle in real life. I certainly never thought I'd fly to one on the back of a giant swan.

We land outside the castle walls. Finola brings us down on a small pond. We jump off just as she hops up onto the shore. Honestly, it feels good to be back on the ground.

"We're very grateful, Finola," Salix says.

"Yes," I say. "Tha—" Salix kicks me. "What?"

"You should never say 'thank you' to a Faerie," he says. "It's insulting."

Finola sniffs and looks away.

"Oh. Okay." That's kind of a weird rule, but what isn't in Faerie land? "I might be able to help you, Finola," I say instead. "I thought of something while we were flying."

Finola looks at me.

"What if I say your full name?" I ask. "If I knew it, I could command you to turn back into a Faerie—or back to your original form. Would that work?"

Finola actually shrugs, ruffling her wings.

"It might work," Salix says. "But all I know is Finola MacLear. Do you have middle names, Finola?"

She suddenly waddles into the trees. Salix and I chase her. When we find her, she is nibbling on a thorn and tapping the trunk of the tree. Over and over.

"Thorn?" I try. "Thorntree?"

She shakes her head.

"Thornwood?" Salix says.

Finola nods. She lifts one wing, spreading her flight feathers out.

"Feathers?" I ask.

She nods again. I can see she's excited. She hops up and down on her webbed feet. All I can do now is try it.

"Finola Thornwood Feathers MacLear," I say. "I command you to return to your original form."

I expect it to happen in a puff of smoke or a flash. That's how magic works in movies and TV. But what actually happens is much worse. Finola's swan body becomes misshapen. It stretches.

Her feathered skin seems to tear. And she honks and hisses like she's in pain. I'm so freaked out I actually close my eyes for a second.

When I open them, a girl is standing there. She's wearing what looks like a white feather bikini. Her hair is long and black, swept back by a feather crown. Her eyes are a very dark brown. She looks to be about the same age as Salix and me.

"Finola!" Salix says. "You look great!"

"I'm half-naked!" she says. "Blue! Can you command me some proper clothes?"

"Oh...uh..." I stumble. What clothes would she want to wear? I'm sure to get it wrong. "Finola Thornwood Feathers MacLear, I command you to clothe yourself in...uh...something sensible," I finally say.

This spell *does* involve smoke. When it clears, Finola is wearing a tunic, leggings and a short cape. She has leather boots and a belt with a sword in a sheath. In short, she looks awesome.

"That's better," she says. "Blue, you have one more wish. Can you use it now so I don't have to worry about it?"

I really want a sword like hers now. But I'd never be allowed to keep it back in the human world. I get an idea.

"Finola Thornwood Feathers MacLear, I command you to give me a real sword and sheath that only I can see!"

Finola smirks at me. At first nothing happens, but then I feel something in my hand. I look down. I'm holding a leather belt with a sheath attached. There's a sword in the sheath!

"Did it work?" Salix asks.

"Wait," I say as I buckle the belt on. It fits perfectly. "You mean you can't see this?"

His face lights up. "No!" he says. "Do you really have an invisible sword? That's amazing!"

"I didn't even know I could make invisible things," Finola says. "I—"

But she's interrupted. There's a noise behind us. Seconds later a dozen armed men smash through the trees.

"Halt in the name of Oren Bramble, King of Farwood!" one of them says. "Put up your hands!"

Oren's soldiers march us through the castle gate. They take Finola's sword. And Salix's lantern. But they don't even bother to frisk me.

"Look at the little human!" one of them says. He laughs. I guess I don't look very threatening.

Inside the castle, we are taken down a dark, winding stairway. The soldiers carry burning torches to light our way. We seem to descend hundreds of feet. Finally we reach the bottom.

It's a dungeon.

"This isn't good," Salix says unhelpfully.

The soldiers lead us along a long passageway.

At the end is a set of bars. One of the soldiers jangles some keys. The bars swing open. The soldiers shove us through. The lock clangs shut behind us.

This cell is quite large. It's about twenty feet wide and at least as long. The walls are very high. Way above us in the gloom, I can just make out two small barred windows. Combined with the torches on the walls outside the bars, they let in a little light.

Something up there moves.

"What's that?" I ask. I'm tempted to draw my invisible sword. But I can't—I don't want the guards to know I have it. I step in front of Salix and Finola.

"Blue?" a soft voice says.

There's more movement up in the gloom. A small shape moves past one of the windows.

"Blue? What are you doing here?" another voice says.

I blink and try to see in the dark as two shapes move down toward us. My fingers twitch over the hilt of my sword. The things coming down have wings!

Oh, wow. It's Indigo and Violet. And they're flying.

As they flutter into the light of the torches, I get a proper look at their wings. Unlike Olea's bat-like ones, these look like butterfly wings. They are large and rounded, blue with black edges, white spots, and curled tips. Indigo's wings are slightly larger than Violet's. Hers are more shimmery. They sparkle in the torchlight.

Indigo is shirtless and barefoot. But he's wearing the shorts I last saw him in. Violet has torn and refashioned her shirt into a halter style so her wings can flap free. She's barefoot too. They both look a bit dirty.

As the twins settle to the floor, their wings retract. Soon they are nothing but vague ripples on their backs. Neither Salix nor Finola seems concerned about this.

"Are you two okay?" I ask. I decide to worry about the wings later. "Has anyone hurt you?"

"We're hungry," the twins say together.

I quickly dig out the granola bars and hand them over. I'm pretty hungry myself, but they're just little kids. As they chew, we all sit down. I introduce the twins to Salix and Finola.

"Do you know why you're here?" I ask them.

"King Oren kidnapped us," Violet says.

"Because he hates our mother," Indigo says.

"Not Mom," Violet adds. "Our other mother. Queen Olea."

"How long have you known you had another mother?" I ask.

Indigo shrugs. "A while," he says.

My ears start to ring again. I have to shake my head to make it stop. If the twins knew about the Faerie Woods and everything, why didn't they tell me? They must have known how much danger all of us were in. Good grief, why were these two always so frustrating?

"Queen Olea killed King Oren's father," Violet says in a calm voice.

"What?" I yell. That is a detail Olea left out of her story.

"It's true," Indigo says. "We heard the guards talking about it. Didn't we?"

Violet nods.

"Why did she kill him?" I ask.

"No one knows," Indigo says. "It was years ago. They had set up a camp in the Crosswood to discuss merging the kingdoms. They were there for weeks and weeks. Then Olea left suddenly. And one of the guards found King Gelso—Gelso Bramble, Oren's father—dead. They found him with silver in his mouth."

Salix and Finola gasp.

"Silver poisons Faeries!" Finola explains to me.

"This is not good," I say. "We need to get—"

But I don't finish. I hear someone marching toward our cell. A large guard appears.

"Let's go!" he says as he jams the key in the lock. The bars swing open.

"Where are we going?" I ask.

"To the Great Hall," the guard says. "King Oren has summoned you."

Chapter Nine

The Great Hall is not the right name for it. It's not really a hall. And even though we seem to be inside a castle, Oren's Great Hall is outside. Or it *seems* to be outside.

Faerie land is very confusing.

The walls of the Great Hall are made up of massive trees. They curve over us to make the ceiling. It's daylight now. Sunlight dapples through the leaves and branches. The floor is made of stone paths crisscrossing grass. We walk behind some guards up the long path to the throne. I notice that one of them has a tail.

I look around, trying not to be too obvious about it. There are dozens of creatures sitting in the hall. Some sit in circles on colorful blankets like they're having a picnic. Others are curled up against the trunks of the trees. I think they're asleep. Some stand as we pass. They watch us curiously.

These are Faeries, I guess. I've never put much thought into what Faeries look like. Or what Faeries don't look like. They don't look like Tinker Bell, for example. None of them are tiny, as far as I can see. Most of them are a least human-sized, if not larger. Some of them have tails, like our guard. Some have horns like a goat's or deer's. A few have wings, mostly leathery ones like Olea's. I do see a Faerie whose wings are gray and feathery like a sparrow's. She looks kind, so I smile at her. She doesn't so much smile back as bare her teeth. They are sharp and pointed, like a shark's. I quickly look away.

At the end of the path, a young man sits on a throne similar to the one Olea had in the forest. He is dressed in a similar way too. He wears a blue, sleeveless tunic that reaches just below his knees. On his feet are gold sandals with laces up his calves. A black-and-white, fur-lined cloak lies open on the throne behind him.

His crown is a pinkish gold and is trimmed with blue stones.

Once we get close enough, I can see he is not much older than I am. A teenager.

When we stop in front of the throne, Salix bows deeply.

"Salix Flapfoot, Destroyer of Rugs," King Oren says. "Which piece of my property are you planning to ruin this time?"

Salix doesn't look up. "I'm sorry, Your Majesty. That spell got out of hand. It won't happen again."

"Hmm," Oren says. "See that it doesn't." He turns to his guards. "Put the prince and princess back into the cage. I doubt anyone wants to climb after them into the trees again."

The twins give me their best innocent faces, as though they would never climb somewhere dangerous and awkward. Yeah, right. One of the guards ushers them into a large ornate cage beside the throne. It looks like a birdcage.

"Let them go," I say angrily.

Oren turns to me. "Ah, Blue Jasper, the human brother. How—" he looks me up and down "—charming."

He doesn't look charmed. I put my hands on my hips. The fingers of my right hand rest on the hilt of the invisible sword.

"You have broken Faerie law," I try, even though I know almost nothing about Faerie law. "You have kidnapped the children of Queen Olea of Nearwood."

"Kidnapping children from the human realm is not against Faerie law," Oren says. "We do it all the time."

That makes me lose my train of thought for a second.

"Indigo and Violet aren't human though!" is what I come up with.

"Doesn't matter," Oren says.

"What do you want them for?" I ask. I'm getting desperate. And I'm getting nowhere, clearly.

Oren softens suddenly, and when I meet his eyes I see they are icy blue. And sad. His whole face looks sad.

"Faerie law is complicated," he says. "Olea killed my father. Had she tried to enter Farwood to do it, the magical treaty would have prevented her. Had she lured him to Nearwood to do it, Faerie law would have prevented it. But she did it in the Crosswood. The magic of the Faerie Woods is now unbalanced.

It knows Olea must pay for what she did. But it doesn't know how. That causes problems."

"What kind of problems?" I ask.

Oren shakes his head. "Magical problems. Things falling into the Faerie realm from the human realm. Last month a beagle fell into my bathtub. Toadstools growing ten feet high in my dining room." He looks pointedly at Salix as he says this. Salix averts his eyes. "The worst thing is that bad magic grows," Oren says. "My kingdom is threatened. Witches gain power they never had before." He turns to Finola. "I see you've broken the bog witch's spell at last."

"Yes, Your Majesty," Finola says.

"What does this have to do with the twins?" I ask.

Oren takes a breath and leans forward in his throne. He fixes his blue eyes on me.

"I have restored balance," he says. "Olea took my father. I took her children."

"What are you going to do with them?"

Oren suddenly seems even sadder. He looks away, shrugging. "Nothing," he says. "Keep them. Hope that is enough to satisfy the Woods."

"And if it's not?" I ask.

"It will be," Finola says. Her voice sounds too small.

I start to panic. I know what no one is saying. If the balance of Faerie Woods isn't restored, Oren will kill the twins. That thought gives me focus like I've never had before. I start talking. Fast.

"What if—okay, I'm a human, right? I'm not constrained by Faerie law. I can get into Nearwood. I can get at Queen Olea. What if I punished her in some other way?" I ask. I'm thinking of my invisible sword. Could I really do that? Kill someone to protect the twins and Mom? *Am I going to have a choice?*

Oren looks almost amused. "How could a human punish a Faerie?" he asks.

I don't want to suggest murder just yet. That seems extreme. And unlikely. I try hard to think of something.

"Silver!" I say. "Mom has some silver jewelry. I could go and get it and give it to Olea somehow. Like... use it to...tie her up?"

No one says anything. I look over at Salix.

"No offense," he says, "but that is a really dumb idea. For starters, we don't have time."

He's right. There's no way I could get home and back again before sunset. That's when Mom's payment for breaking the pact with Olea comes due. That's when Faerie magic will kill her.

I really hate Faerie land.

Chapter Ten

There's only one thing left to try. I know Oren isn't human, but I'm going to try to appeal to his humanity. It's all I have. Unless I want to bust out the invisible sword.

Which I don't.

I go down on one knee. "King Oren," I start. But I find it hard to say what I want to. "I know how hard it is to lose a father," I finally get out. "My father left me when I was just a baby. Since then it's just been my mom and me. And the twins."

I don't know what I expect. Maybe some sympathetic looks. A couple of tears. Oren just looks confused.

"The twins' human father doesn't live with you?" Oren says.

Now I'm confused. Why would he ask that? And what does he mean by human father?

"No," I say. "I don't know who their father is. I don't think they know either." I turn to the twins, who are watching, wide-eyed, from their cage. "Do you?" I ask them.

"No, Blue," they answer together.

Oren frowns. His body language changes. He seems angry now. "The twins' human father has never lived with you?" he asks through his teeth.

"Not that I know of. Who told you he did? Olea?"

Oren stands. "Your mother told me," he says. "She told me the first time I tried to take the twins from her. Magic stopped me, but I was able to ask a few questions. Your mother told me the twins' father was her human husband. That he had been with Olea before they met. That Olea sent him away from Faerie land to be with the twins. And that he married your mother."

"Mom told you all this?"

Oren sits back down with a huff. "Yes," he says tightly. "I do not like to be told lies."

The word *lies* hangs in my head. Lies. I remember Salix telling me that Faeries can't tell lies. But humans can. In fact, we do it all the time. Olea must have asked Mom to lie about the twins' father. But why would she do that? It seems pointless.

Unless she didn't want Oren to know who the twins' father really is.

Or *was*.

I get a chill. The hair on the back of my neck prickles. Oren is glaring down at me.

"I do not like to be told lies by *humans*," he says.

I think I know why Olea wanted Mom to lie. I hope I'm right. I hope Faeries can't read minds. I also hope what I'm about to do is not crazy.

"Is it against Faerie law to have a human lie on your behalf?" I ask.

Oren makes a face. "I don't know," he says. "If it's not, it should be."

"Maybe Queen Olea knows," I say. "At the very least you should ask her why she wanted my mother to lie."

Maybe if Olea comes here, I can push her into attacking Oren. I can defend him with my sword. Then he'll owe me his life, and I can take the twins instead.

It's a dumb plan, but it's the only one I have.

Oren stares at me for a long time. Finally he nods. "I'm curious now," he admits. "If Olea is having humans lie for her, there's a *real* story. I'd like to know what it is." He stands, reaching for an ornate staff by his throne. He raises it up and bangs it on the stone floor three times. With each bang a bright spark shoots out from the top of the staff. The sparks fly up into the trees as Oren speaks.

"Olea of Nearwood," he says loudly. "I invite you to Farwood, to my court. Come alone!" Then he tosses the staff down and sits.

"Uh…okay," I say. "When will she be here?"

"Soon," Oren says.

$$\Rightarrow \star \Leftarrow$$

I sit with Finola and Salix as we wait. Oren has lost interest in us. He is flirting with a pink-haired Faerie girl.

"You have some kind of bonkers human plan, don't you?" Finola asks me. She is grinning. I get the feeling she enjoys bonkers human plans.

"It's bonkers, all right," I admit. "But I don't know how human it is."

"Don't tell us about it," Salix says. "If it goes wrong

or something happens, we can't lie about it to save you. Or ourselves."

"Good thinking," Finola says. "The less we know, the better."

Not exactly the kind of support I was hoping for.

Just then the ground starts to rumble. Faeries sitting around the throne stand and move out of the way. Finola, Salix and I join them. Oren sits up on his throne, shoving the pink-haired girl away. The twins poke their heads through the bars of their cage, straining to see.

The stone in front of the throne cracks. The noise makes me jump. The two pieces of stone move apart, and a pair of feet appears, roots and earth churning around them. Oren watches, mildly interested. But when two more pairs of feet appear, he signals his guards. They come forward, swords drawn.

I arrived in the Crosswood in pretty much the same way. Upside down through the earth. I didn't realize how clumsy it looks. Olea's skirt tangles around her legs as the roots push her up. She finally emerges, pulling her head out of the dirt. She jumps to her feet just as her guards pull themselves up too. They draw their swords.

I think this all must be for show. Surely Oren's guards and Olea's guards and all these swords are just for show. Right?

Wrong.

Olea raises her sword and dives for Oren. His guards are so busy with Olea's guards, they can't defend him. Oren dashes out of the way just in time. He grabs his staff and blocks Olea's sword. Both of them change as they fight. Olea becomes taller. Her wings spread out, green and shiny. Her beautiful face twists into a snarl of teeth and glowing yellow eyes. Oren raises himself up. His face becomes covered with sharp-looking designs like tattoos. His wings spread out too. They are blue and black and—

I *knew* it.

Suddenly Oren's staff splinters under Olea's blade. He manages to kick her, and she tumbles backward.

One of Oren's guards is now down, wounded. The other one is fighting Olea's two men. Everyone is screaming. Oren is backing away from Olea. She stalks after him, sword raised.

"How dare you attack me in my own court!" Oren says, furious. "You have no honor."

"I don't need honor," Olea says. "I have a crown."

Her sword flies down. Suddenly I'm leaping forward, drawing my own sword from the sheath at my waist. I raise it just in time to stop Olea from slicing Oren in two.

Our swords make a huge clang as they crash together. Sparks fly all around us.

"What magic is this?" Olea says. She presses down on my sword. She is much stronger than me. Oren has scrambled away. Now I'm Olea's target.

"Human boy," she says. "You should not meddle in Faerie affairs."

She shoves down, knocking me to the ground. I'm still blocking her, but barely. I have only one thing left to try. If this doesn't work, I die.

"Olea Nash Panash Buckthorn Briar—" I yell.

Olea's eyes widen in horror.

"—Bramble!" I finish.

She gasps.

"Olea Nash Panash Buckthorn Briar Bramble, I command you!" I shout. "Drop your sword!"

Chapter Eleven

Olea starts to scream. Her scream makes the trees and ground tremble. The air trembles. Faeries run for their lives as the scream goes on for what seems like forever. Olea's terrifying, snarling face is inches from mine. The blade of her sword pushes my own sword back until I feel the steel just touch my neck.

Then Olea rears backward. There's a flash of bright light as her sword flies out of her hand. Behind her I see Salix leap up and snatch it out of the air. In the shock of the scream and the bright light, Oren's guards have managed to subdue Olea's men.

Silence settles over the court. Everyone stares at me. I'm sure they're wondering what I'll do next. I wonder too. I can't move yet. I'm gasping for breath as I struggle to stand up. Behind me, I hear the king speak.

"Blue Jasper," he says. "Where did you get a ghost sword?"

I'm not sure if I should tell him. Maybe it's against Faerie law or something. I'm already in enough trouble. I look at Finola and Salix, but they are speechless.

"It's a long story," I say. I turn to Oren, expecting him to be angry. But he's smiling.

"I should like to have a sword like that," he says.

I fumble putting the sword back into its sheath. My vision blurs as I undo the buckle of the belt. Stepping forward, I hold it out to Oren.

"Take it," I say. I'm shaking so bad the sword rattles in my hand. "Take it, please."

Oren frowns at me. "Are you sure?" he asks.

"Yes." My voice is barely above a whisper. "I never want to hold a sword again."

Oren nods slowly and takes the sword and sheath out of my hand. As soon as he does, it disappears from my view. I think he sets it down on the throne beside him. Then he reaches forward and puts his hand on my shoulder. With his other hand he takes a blue handkerchief from his pocket. I grab it quickly and wipe my eyes.

"No one saw but me," he says with a small smile.

I take a second to gather myself. Oren squeezes my shoulder.

"Do you want to unite Nearwood and Farwood?" I whisper.

Oren looks surprised, but he nods.

"Yes, I do," he says in a low voice. "As did my father before me. And his father. Our people have hated each other long enough."

For some reason that makes me think of Indigo and Violet and how they annoy me with their antics. And how I love them with all my heart. I find I have to wipe my eyes again. Oren releases my shoulder.

"You have two more commands," he says, flicking his eyes to where Olea lies crumpled on the ground.

I nod. I know exactly what to do. It feels like the first time in my life that I have. As I turn, Olea sits up.

"Olea Nash Panash Buckthorn Briar Bramble," I say with as much severity as I can manage. "I command you to answer this question. Is the father of your twins, Indigo and Violet, also the father of Oren, King of Farwood? Is their father Gelso Bramble?"

There are horrified gasps. Olea's face twists with fury.

"Yes," she spits out.

→ ★ ←

Oren stands. "Is this true?" he asks. "Indigo and Violet are my brother and sister? Olea of Nearwood, are you telling the truth?"

"Faeries cannot lie," Olea says bitterly.

Oren spins to his guards. "Let them out of the cage!" he commands.

A guard turns the lock of the cage, and Indigo and Violet step out, holding each other.

"Approach me," Oren says. "Let me look at you."

The twins stand in front of him. I can tell they're scared. But not *that* scared. These are the kids that jumped out of the back of a moving truck, after all.

"Show him your wings," I say.

Indigo and Violet shiver for a few seconds, as though they have been chilled. Then their wings shimmer into view behind them. Blue and black butterfly wings. Just like Oren's.

"Oh my stars above," Oren says. He rushes forward and gathers them into his arms. He kisses them each on the forehead. "Brother. Sister," he says. After a few seconds, the twins squirm away.

"Can we sit on the throne?" Violet asks.

Oren laughs. "Please do!" he says. But when he turns back to Olea, his mood has darkened.

"Tell me how this came to be," he says. "I note you were commanded by my family name—Bramble. Does that mean you and my father were married?"

"Yes," Olea hisses.

"Stand before the king!" Finola suddenly says. "You are a guest of this court!"

Olea sneers at her, but she stands up.

"Yes, Gelso and I secretly married in the Crosswood," she says to Oren. "A wandering priestess performed the ceremony. Gelso wanted us to rule the Woods together as husband and wife."

I can see Oren is feeling the loss of his father. His eyes fill with tears.

"Why in the name of the sky was that not enough for you? Why, why, did you kill him?"

"I didn't want to share power!" Olea shouts.

"Why on earth not?" I ask without thinking. When Oren doesn't react, I go on, "The Woods are enormous and…" But I trail off, not knowing what I want to say.

Olea laughs sourly. "A *human* telling me about sharing territory? That *is* amusing."

She has a point. I press my lips together.

"I discovered I was pregnant," she says. "I knew my child could be the ruler of the Woods and I their adviser. It would be as good as being High Queen of both Woods myself. But when I bore twins…"

She looks at the twins with resentment in her eyes. I suddenly know she never loved them. At least, not the way Mom does. Not the way I do.

"With twins, I knew Gelso would suggest that one rule Farwood and one Nearwood," Olea says. "I would have even less power than I already had."

Oren takes a step toward her. "So you sent them away," he says. "You killed my father and sent away his children. My brother and sister." One of his hands is clenched. I realize he is holding the ghost sword. As much as I hate Olea right now, I don't want to see her killed. I do the only thing I can think of.

"Olea Nash Panash Buckthorn Briar Bramble, I command you!"

A hush falls over the hall. All eyes turn to me, including Oren's. I need to get this right.

"I...I command you to relinquish the throne of Nearwood in favor of Violet Nash Panash Buckthorn Briar Bramble!"

"No!" Olea shouts, her eyes filled with horror.

"I command you!" I repeat. "Give Violet your crown!"

Olea bends over, clutching her stomach as though she is in pain.

"No! I cannot!" she cries. "I will not!"

"I COMMAND YOU!" I shout. It echoes through the trees. The magic of the Woods rises up around us, causing everything to rumble like an earthquake. Olea screams and falls backward, like something has pushed her. Her crown flies off her head and sails through the air. It lands neatly on Violet's head, settling there as though it was made for her.

Now the hall is completely silent. Indigo clambers off the throne, leaving Violet there by herself. She looks different. Older and wiser. When she looks at Olea, I take a step back. I've never seen Violet so angry.

"Olea Briar," she says. "You have killed our father, the King of Farwood. You have threatened our foster mother, Juliette Jasper. You have endangered our brother, Blue Jasper. You have drawn a sword against King Oren in his own court. You have broken the laws of the Woods. All pacts with you are hereby made null. You are hereafter and ever after banished to Witherwood."

"No!" Olea cries. "You can't!"

"I can," Violet says. "And I do. King Oren, do you agree?"

"Yes, Your Majesty," says Oren.

Olea screams as the roots beneath her feet curl up around her ankles. She shouts curses, but the roots pull her down into the soil. Her mouth fills with dirt, and her cries are muffled by the earth closing over her head. In seconds she is gone.

It takes a while for me to be able to speak.

"What is Witherwood?" I ask.

"It is the place bad Faeries go," Oren says.

Chapter Twelve

Violet and Indigo have been spending weekdays in the Faerie realm. They spend weekends with us. So far, it's been a month. It's working well. Mom has a part-time job in town. I've started high school. Life is back to normal.

"Indigo!" Mom yells from the kitchen. "Don't open your wings in the house! You nearly knocked over the dish rack!"

Normal except for that.

I'm just putting away my clean socks when I see Salix and Finola outside my window. They wave at me.

"We'll be right out!" I yell.

Salix and Finola come to get the twins every Sunday night. They take them back through the Crosswood. King Oren thinks it best if I stay away from Nearwood and Farwood for the time being. Olea is definitely imprisoned in Witherwood. Permanently. But she might still have supporters in the Woods. Oren and Violet need to secure Violet's reign. Then it will be safe for Mom and me to visit.

In the kitchen, Mom struggles to put a hoodie on Indigo. He doesn't want to fold up his wings. Violet has a cooking pot on her head and one hand in the jam jar. Business as usual.

Five minutes later I take them out the back door. Salix and Finola meet us. We head down the path into the forest. I can almost hear Mom collapsing on the sofa, exhausted.

"How is Oren?" I ask as we walk. The twins, as usual, bounce along the path ahead of us.

"He's fine," Salix says. "He managed to get the toadstools out of his rug!"

"That's good," I say, trying not to laugh.

"The people of Nearwood are happy with Violet as their queen," Finola says. "They didn't like Olea much. She was cruel."

"Violet is easy to like," I say.

Oren meets us in the grove with the twisted trees.

"All well, Blue Jasper?" he asks.

"All well," I say. "The twins are little maniacs, as usual."

Oren laughs. "I wouldn't want it any other way," he says.

It still makes me nervous to come here. This is where Indigo and Violet disappeared the first time. Now this is where they'll leave me for another week.

They hug me before they go. After they disappear into the twisted trees, I realize Violet took the coins from my pocket. Indigo put a spider in my hair. They both left jammy handprints on my shirt.

Salix and Finola snicker as I turn.

"I suppose you should go too," I say.

"Salix has something he wants to ask you," Finola says, grinning.

"Okay," I say cautiously. Salix and Finola are my friends. But with Faeries, even ones that are friends, it pays to be cautious.

"You still owe me a favor," Salix says.

"Oh no," I say.

"I promised it wouldn't be bad!" Salix says quickly. "And it isn't. Remember how I told you about the place I'm from?"

"Yes," I say. "You said the way into it had disappeared."

"That's right," Salix says. "But recently there have been rumors it's been found again."

"That's great!" I say. "You can go home!"

Finola grins and covers her mouth.

"It's very far away," Salix says.

"You can make it," I say.

"I'll be lonely on the journey," Salix says.

"Finola can go with you."

Both of them just grin at me.

"No," I say.

"Come on," Finola says. "It will be much more fun with the three of us."

"No way," I say. "Mom will kill me."

"I already told her you'd made a deal with me," Salix says. "She didn't take it well."

"Salix!" I shout. "I thought we were friends!"

He shrugs, trying to look innocent. "Friendship with Faeries is always a bit tricky," he says.

"You think?" I let my face fall into my hands.

"Please, Blue," Salix says, now serious. "There is magic that only works with a human helper. We might need you. Remember how you broke the bog witch's spell? You turned Finola back into herself?"

I look at them both. "I can't go like this," I say. "I don't even have a jacket."

Finola reaches over and pulls back the branches of a shrub. My backpack is there. A hoodie is neatly folded on top of it.

"Your mom even packed snacks," Finola says. "Cupcakes!"

"Oh my…argh!" I throw up my hands. "Fine!" Finola and Salix cheer as I slip on my hoodie and backpack.

"Where are we going and how long will we be gone?" I ask.

"The Crosswood first," Salix says. "Then we have to walk. For a few days."

"A few days?" I cry. "What about school?"

"Eh," Salix says. "You can miss a week."

"Or a month," Finola says. Salix shushes her.

I just shake my head. "Let's get going," I say. I'm pretending to be angry. Really, I'm excited to get back to Faerie land. High school isn't nearly as interesting as I thought it would be.

Finola leads us into the tangled trees.

"Now," Salix says. "A few safety tips."

"I know, I know," I say. "Rule one: Never make deals with Faeries."

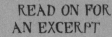

Chapter Three

The breakfast feast is nearly as big as the dinner feast. Finola and Salix stuff themselves on little blue eggs and bright purple porridge. Oren gives me a box of toaster waffles. Then he uses magic to make a tiny fire in a teacup. I toast my waffles over it with a fork.

Two servants bring me a giant silver tray. There is a small can of orange soda on it. Everyone watches me drink it. They cheer when the bubbles make me burp.

Mealtimes are weird in Faerieland.

After breakfast Oren sees us off at the castle gate. He has decided Indigo will go with us.

"I've looked at the Faerie laws," Oren says. "Blue will go with Salix to the entrance of the Wherewood. I believe the Woods will see that as your pact fulfilled." He frowns at Indigo. "After that, Indigo will take Blue back to the human realm. While he's there he will stop in at…" He turns to one of his guards. "What is the name of that place?"

"Garden Depot," the guard whispers.

Oren nods. " Ah yes. Indigo will stop at Garden Depot and buy me a new rose bush."

Salix laughs. He quickly covers it by pretending to cough.

While Finola and Salix check their supplies, Oren takes me aside. When no one is looking, he presses something into my hand. I look down.

A sword and scabbard shimmer into view. The ghost sword!

The ghost sword is visible only to the person using it. Back when Finola was a swan, I commanded her by using her full name. She had to give me three wishes. I used one wish to turn her back into a human. Then I commanded her some new clothes. Finally I asked her for an invisible sword. That was the ghost sword. I used it to help defeat Olea. But I didn't like it. I really don't like any kind of violence.

I had given the ghost sword to Oren. Now he was giving it back to me.

"A loan," he says. "I hope you won't need to use it. You'll only be in Farwood and the Crosswood, but still. I want you to be safe. Indigo can bring the sword back to me when you're done."

"Thank you," I whisper.

We set off, slipping by magic back into the Crosswood. Then we continue on foot. Hours pass. Indigo chatters away about nothing. I notice that

Salix and Finola sometimes hold hands as they walk.

"Are you two together?" I finally ask. "Like a couple?"

"Yes," says Salix

"No," says Finola.

"Never mind," I say.

Indigo snorts with laughter. It's nice to see that romance is just as dumb in Faerieland as it is in the human world.

It's nearly dusk when Salix spots something in the dense trees.

"There it is!" he cries.

Indigo starts running.

"Stop!" I yell, chasing after him.

He's still ahead of me when we reach a clearing in the trees. On the other side of the clearing is an old VW van. It's tangled in a dense hedge. It looks a lot like the one Mom used to have. Hers was pale blue. This one is bright yellow.

Indigo yanks open the passenger door. He climbs in.

"No, Indigo!" Finola yells.

The door slams closed behind him.

The three of us arrive at the clearing together. Salix and Finola trip on a tree root. They both go flying. I keep running. When I reach the van, I tug the door open.

"Indigo!" I yell. It's dark inside the van. Indigo is probably hiding. I climb in after him. The door slams behind me. The door on the other side of the van opens. Indigo is standing outside. The forest around him looks different. I don't pay much attention to it though. I jump out and grab his arm.

"Don't run off like that," I say angrily. Last time Indigo ran off (with Violet) Oren kidnapped him. And Olea nearly killed Mom and me. I'd rather not repeat that.

I turn to drag him back through the van.

But the van is gone.

Gabrielle Prendergast is an award-winning author who has written a number of books for young people, including *Audacious*, winner of the Westchester Award, *Zero Repeat Forever*, winner of the Sheila A. Egoff Prize for Children's Literature, and *Pandas on the Eastside*, which was shortlisted for the Chocolate Lily Award, the Red Cedar Award, the Diamond Willow Award and the Vancouver Book Award. She has an MFA in creative writing from the University of British Columbia and has taught writing at Sydney University, San Francisco State University, UBC and Royal Canadian College. She lives in Vancouver.